BIONICLE™

The
Darkness Below

BIONICLE™

FIND THE POWER,
LIVE THE LEGEND

The legend comes alive in these exciting BIONICLE™ books:

BIONICLE™ Chronicles
#1 Tale of the Toa
#2 Beware the Bohrok
#3 Makuta's Revenge
#4 Tales of the Masks

The Official Guide to BIONICLE™

BIONICLE™ Collector's Sticker Book

BIONICLE™: Mask of Light

BIONICLE™ Adventures
#1 Mystery of Metru Nui
#2 Trial by Fire

BIONICLE™

The Darkness Below

by Greg Farshtey

SCHOLASTIC INC.
New York Toronto London Auckland Sydney
Mexico City New Delhi Hong Kong Buenos Aires

*For Leah, who brings style, class,
and grace to everything she does*

ISBN 0-439-60733-7

12 11 10 9 8 7 6 5 4 3 2   4 5 6 7 8 9/0

Printed in the U.S.A.
First printing, June 2004

INTRODUCTION

Jaller paused from his labors for a moment and took a deep breath. He could not remember ever working harder than he had in the past few days. Ever since it had been announced that the Matoran were going to move from the island of Mata Nui to the island city of Metru Nui, villagers had been toiling day and night to build enough boats for the great journey.

For Jaller and his friends, the nonstop work was welcome. Their home, Ta-Koro, had been destroyed in the battle to save the island from darkness, and they were living in other villages until the time came to leave Mata Nui forever. Talk around the fires at night was about Metru Nui, what wonders they might find there, and how soon they would be able to leave for this new and mysterious place.

"We'll never get to Metru Nui if the great Jaller keeps taking rest breaks."

Jaller turned to see his friend Hahli smiling at him. The Ga-Matoran had recently been named the new Chronicler, and ever since she had been traveling from place to place gathering tales about Metru Nui. She hoped to be able to share the stories with the other Matoran during the long journey to come.

"At least when I'm working, I'm *working,*" replied Jaller good-naturedly. "You can't build a boat with a story, you know."

"Maybe not, but it sure makes the sailing go faster. I'm heading to see Turaga Vakama. He's about to continue his tale of Metru Nui to the Toa. I am supposed to record it for the Wall of History we will build on the new island. Come with me?"

Jaller thought about it. He probably should keep working, but he was already far ahead of all the others. It wouldn't do any harm to take a little time off.

"Okay. Let's go," he said.

The two of them set out for the Amaja Circle sandpit, the place where Turaga Vakama traditionally told his tales. After a short while, Jaller asked, "So is it true?"

"Is what true?"

"All the stories I have been hearing. How the Turaga were once Toa on Metru Nui; how they searched for six missing Matoran, but learned that one of the Matoran planned to betray the city; and how they gathered six Great Disks and used them to defeat a menace called the Morbuzakh."

Hahli nodded. "Yes, it's all true. Amazing, isn't it? One moment, they were Matoran just like us, living and working in a great city. The next moment, they were Toa Metru with powers and Toa tools and everything!"

Up ahead, they could see the seven Toa gathered around Turaga Vakama. The Turaga had already begun to speak. "It had been a difficult and dangerous mission, but we six Toa Metru had triumphed. Metru Nui had been saved from the Morbuzakh, and we were certain that we would be hailed as heroes. But we were about to face another test, one that would threaten to shatter our newfound unity."

The Turaga of Fire turned his gaze to the night sky, but all present knew that his eyes were truly viewing images from the past. "Toa would challenge Toa in the darkness below the city, in a struggle that still lives in my nightmares."

The six Toa Metru walked through the streets of Ta-Metru, on their way to the Coliseum. For the first time since they had transformed from Matoran, they felt no need to travel by way of back alleys or to stay in the shadows. Even the presence of Vahki, Metru Nui's order enforcement squads, did not worry them. After all, they had just defeated the Morbuzakh plant that menaced the city. They were heroes!

Better still, they had found the legendary Great Disks, which had been hidden in separate parts of the city. They had no doubt that these artifacts would be enough to convince the city's elder, Turaga Dume, and all the Matoran that here were new Toa capable of defeating any threat.

"They will cheer-hail us in the Coliseum," said Matau, Toa of Air, with a grin. "Po-Metru carvers will make statues of us. Perhaps they will even rename the districts for us! 'Ma-Metru' — I like the ring-sound of that!"

The other Toa laughed. Matau was exaggerating, of course, but certainly Turaga Dume would honor them in some way. Matoran all over the city would demand it.

"With the Morbuzakh gone, maybe we won't have any dangers to face," offered Whenua, Toa of Earth. "Except for the occasional Rahi beast on the loose, Metru Nui is usually pretty peaceful."

"Just rest on our reputations, huh, Whenua?" said Onewa, Toa of Stone. "Not me. Now that I'm a Toa Metru, I'm going to take advantage of it. The best tools, the best materials, mine for the asking — I'll build statues like you have never seen before!"

"I will do many Toa-hero deeds," said Matau. "That way there will always be tales to tell about me. What about you, Nokama?"

"Well, I'm not sure," replied the Toa of Water. "There are so many places to see and explore. What is it like under the sea? What lies beyond the sky? Where do all those strange creatures you see in the Onu-Metru Archives come from? Now I have the power to go wherever I please and learn those answers."

Nuju, Toa of Ice, shrugged. "I don't feel any need to explore. I have more than enough to keep me busy in Ko-Metru. Now that I am a Toa, perhaps others will not be so quick to interrupt me when I am working."

Only Vakama, Toa of Fire, had yet to speak. Of all the Toa Metru, he was the least comfortable with his new powers and the responsibilities that came with them. Still, when duty demanded it, he had risen to the occasion and led the Toa to victory. Nokama noticed his silence and asked, "What about you, Vakama? Surely you have some dream you want to realize now that you are a Toa?"

"Not really," he answered. "I mean, I am glad we became Toa and were able to save the city. But . . . I would be just as happy to still be working at my forge in Ta-Metru. It was much simpler. I guess once a mask-maker, always a mask-maker."

Onewa chuckled. "The fire-spitter wants to go back to being a Matoran. I don't think the transformation works in the opposite direction."

"Yes, we are stuck being Toa-heroes," said Matau. "And so many worry-problems we have — how many bows to take? How many mask-sculptures in each metru? How big of a shelter-house for each of us?"

"If you aren't happy being a Toa, Vakama, maybe we should choose a new leader," said Onewa. "I am sure I could do the job."

"Or I!" said Matau. "Matau of Ma-Metru, leader of the Toa-heroes! Oh, I like that!"

"I never said I didn't want to be a Toa," Vakama said. "And I *never* said I wanted to be the leader. I did the job because I knew Ta-Metru better than any of you. If someone else wants to be leader, go ahead."

Nokama looked at Vakama. She could tell that he was hurt by the things Onewa and Matau were saying, but he wasn't going to admit to it. As they walked, the other Toa Metru debated who was best qualified to lead the team. Onewa said it should be a creative thinker like him. Matau countered that a high-flyer was best qualified to plan strategy. Whenua said he would take the job if asked, then seemed disappointed when no one asked him.

As for Nuju, the Toa of Ice summed up his feelings in a few words. "I don't care who leads us, as long as he doesn't expect me to follow."

Nokama was about to put all four of them in their place when she saw a Matoran approaching at a run. He was from Onu-Metru, and the anxious look on his face said there was serious trouble somewhere.

Whenua stepped forward to greet him. The Matoran's name was Nuparu, and he was not someone Whenua knew well. When other workers in the Archives were busy among the exhibits, Nuparu was off on his own tinkering. He was always trying to figure out how Gukko birds flew, how the great Muaka cat could stretch its neck to lunge at prey, and other questions that might seem trivial to others. Still, Nuparu leaving the Archives and hurrying into Ta-Metru was enough to catch the Toa of Earth's attention.

"Toa! The Archives are in danger!" the Matoran shouted.

"It's all right, Nuparu," said Whenua. "The Morbuzakh has been defeated. Everyone is safe."

The Matoran shook his head frantically. "No, no, it's not the Morbuzakh. It's the sea! It's going to flood the Archives and destroy all of the exhibits!"

Whenua wasn't sure how to react to the Matoran's words. The Onu-Metru digging machines, and the workers who operated them, took special care to make sure the outer walls of the Archives were reinforced. The deeper they dug to create new sublevels, the greater the pressure from the liquid protodermis outside. But the sea had never posed a serious threat to the existence of the exhibits in all of Metru Nui's recorded history.

The Toa of Earth waved the other Toa Metru away. This was an Onu-Metru problem, and would be solved by the guardian of that district, he decided. "Now tell me what you saw," he said to Nuparu.

"I was down . . . um . . . below the sublevels, and —"

"Wait a moment, what were you doing so far down? You know how risky it is to go there!" As soon as he said it, Whenua regretted the sharpness of his tone. But it had not been so long ago that he had been down in that dark and fearsome section, and he had barely escaped intact. No Onu-Matoran, archivist or not, had any business wandering among "exhibits" deemed too dangerous for display.

"Well, I . . . I . . . I heard there was a Rahkshi down there, a yellow one, and it had been defeated, and I wanted to . . . well . . ."

"You were hoping to scavenge some parts for your latest invention," Whenua finished for him, frowning. "You know what would happen if the other archivists caught you doing that? Or worse, a Vahki?"

"I know," Nuparu said, looking down at his

feet. "But I didn't find anything anyway. Then I saw a hatch in the floor and I went down through it. There was a whole maze of tunnels there I never knew existed! So I used my lightstone to explore. I didn't see very much, no exhibits or anything, but when I rounded a corner, I was suddenly walking in protodermis! The sea was leaking in!"

Nuparu's voice was loud enough that the other Toa Metru could not help but hear. Nokama, in particular, was intrigued by the mention of the sea. She drew closer as the Matoran continued to talk.

"So at first I didn't know what to think. I was going to turn back, but then I figured as long as I was down there, I'd better find out how serious the situation was. I found one whole wall had a huge crack and the sea was pouring right through it!"

"How bad?"

"The crack is spreading. If it's not repaired soon, the whole sea wall will breach," said Nuparu. "The sublevels will flood, then the lower levels, and pretty soon the whole Archives will be washed away."

"But there is a repair crew headed down now, right?"

Nuparu shook his head. "No one wants to go down there. They've all heard too many stories. That's why, when I heard there was a new Toa of Earth, I came looking for you. Someone has to do something!"

"Someone will," replied Whenua. "Now tell me the story again. I want to hear every detail of what you saw, and where you saw it."

Nokama had rejoined the others by the time Whenua was finished talking with the Matoran. The Toa of Earth looked grim as he walked over to the group.

"I have to go," he said. "Someone will have to apologize to Turaga Dume for me, but this is an emergency. I'll meet you all at the Coliseum later on."

"What could be more serious-matter than telling the world what we can do?" asked Matau.

"Actually doing it," Nokama answered. "But you don't have to take on this task alone. I will come with you. The Archives are important to everyone in Metru Nui. I know anyone from Ga-Metru would do the same."

"I'll come too," said Vakama. "My flame power is weak after the struggle with the Mor-buzakh, but maybe I can help somehow." He turned to Onewa. "Can you three explain to Turaga Dume why we cannot present ourselves to him just yet?"

"Oh, sure," Onewa snorted. "'The other three of us would be here, Turaga, but they're out being heroes while we stand around.' I say we *all* go, we *all* do the job, and then we *all* head to the Coliseum. What do you think? Matau? Nuju?"

"The sooner we take care of all this, the sooner I can get back to Ko-Metru," said Nuju. "I say we help Whenua."

"Hmmmmmm," Matau said. "I was in a hurry to tell the Matoran we are Toa-heroes now. But I suppose repair-saving the Archives along with the whole city will be good for twice the celebration. On to Onu-Metru!"

Their course of action agreed upon, the six changed direction and began journeying toward the metru of the archivists. Whenua led the way, still talking with Nuparu, while Nokama and Vakama brought up the rear. After a short while, the Toa of Water said, "You know, we cannot take a vote every time we have to decide something."

"What's that?"

"Just now. The protodermis could have risen another level in the time it took for each Toa to decide if he was coming along or not. We don't have the luxury of debating every point. We need a leader."

"I'm sure you'll do a fine job," he said.

"No, that's not what I —" Nokama began, but the Toa of Fire had already walked away.

Whenua led the Toa Metru to a desolate spot just inside the border of Onu-Metru. Most of the chutes and much of the aboveground structure of the Archives had been damaged by Morbuzakh vines, and Onu-Matoran were now hard at work doing repairs. All of them stopped their labors at the sight of the Toa and crowded around.

Matau greeted them warmly and immediately launched into a tale of the Toa's heroic deeds. The other Toa watched, amused, as he turned their clash with the Morbuzakh into an even greater adventure than it had been.

"If he wasn't a Toa, he could apply to be Chronicler," Onewa said. "Is he ever quiet?"

"Not that you would notice," said Nokama. "Whenua, I don't see an entrance to the Archives here. How will we get where we have to go?"

"There's no entrance you can see," Whenua said. He walked down an alleyway and knelt beside an iron ring in the pavement. He grabbed the ring and, with a mighty heave, pulled open a trapdoor. Tiny winged Rahi and swarms of insects flew up, followed by a wave of damp, foul-smelling air.

"Not very pleasant, I will agree, but it is a shortcut," Whenua said with a shrug. "According to Nuparu, the damage is in the maintenance tunnels. The nickname for them is 'Fikou web,' after what the spiders leave down below, because the tunnels crisscross and twist around each other so."

"What if one of us gets lost?" asked Nokama.

"Don't," replied Whenua. "Just . . . don't. You wouldn't like it. The Matoran tell stories about repair crews that have been wandering down there since the early days of the Archives, unable to find their way out. They are supposed to have gone a little crazy. But, of course, those are just stories."

None of the Toa looked especially comforted by this. Matau had finally finished his tale and came over carrying six lightstones. "Just in case it is night-dark down there."

"Can I come?" asked Nuparu. "I can lead you right to the leak."

"You've done enough already," said Whenua. "I want you to go warn the archivists about this. Tell them we are going to do our best to fix the damage, but they should prepare to move exhibits out of the sub-basements in case they flood. Understand?"

Nuparu nodded and ran off. He understood why Whenua did not want him to come along, but it still frustrated him. As he rushed to carry out the Toa's instructions, he made a vow that someday he would invent something that would help Matoran better defend their homes from danger.

Whenua turned back to his friends, saying, "Hopefully, this won't take long. But be careful. There are always surprises in the Archives."

One by one, the Toa followed him down into the shaft. Only Matau seemed to hesitate, prompting Nokama to turn back and say, "What's the matter?"

"I do not like the below-ground," answered the Toa of Air. "I am a wind-flyer. Toa-hero adventures should only be on the surface, don't you think?"

"We can only hope," said Nokama as she vanished into the darkness.

The maintenance tunnels were to the underground what chutes were to the rest of Metru Nui: a quick means of transport from one end of the city to the other. Unlike chutes, which served everyone in Metru Nui, the tunnels were open only to those with authorization, normally Ta-Matoran and Onu-Matoran. Pipes big and small lined the walls of the tunnels, funneling liquid protodermis from place to place and molten protodermis to those locations that required extra heat.

Ordinarily, Matoran traveled through these tunnels by cart. But Matoran carts were too small for Toa Metru. Whenua idly wondered if the Toa should see about getting vehicles made for them in the future. Might save a lot of walking, swinging, and climbing.

The Toa of Earth felt uneasy. He knew the other Toa Metru were expecting him to take the lead on this mission, but his knowledge of the Fikou web was based largely on stories he had heard. He had never had cause to go much farther than the very outer edges of the tunnel network, and even that was with reluctance.

He was still worrying over this when he felt a cold breeze rush past him. It had come from deep in the maze, which made no sense — there should have been no openings to the outside up ahead. The only hatchways led up to the Archives, and certainly no breeze could come from there.

None of the other Toa seemed particularly disturbed by the strange wind or the drop in temperature. Whenua guessed they just didn't grasp the strangeness of the situation. He suddenly felt as if he could not take another step forward. Something was waiting up ahead, something far worse than any crack in the seawall, and they were walking right into its jaws. He just knew it.

His suspicions were confirmed a few moments later when a thick fog sprang from nowhere to engulf the Toa. Even their lightstones were of little use in penetrating the cloud. Whenua turned to find he could not make out any of his companions.

"Vakama? Nuju? Are you there?" he called out.

"Yes. What is this?" Vakama replied.

"I have never seen fog like this, not even in Ga-Metru," Nokama's voice added. "It is unnatural."

Just how unnatural it was became painfully obvious. A sudden flash of light almost blinded the Toa. An instant later, an impact sent Whenua crashing into his friends. Barely clinging to consciousness, the Toa of Earth said, "What in the name of Mata Nui was that?"

"A lightning bolt," answered Onewa. "A lightning bolt in an enclosed tunnel underground.

Is this normal in Onu-Metru, or are we just lucky?"

As if the freak storm had heard him, a second bolt flew toward the Toa of Stone. Acting on reflex, Onewa dove to the side as the bolt struck the wall where he had been.

"That was no accident," said Nokama. "Perhaps it's time we turned back and planned a strategy."

Nuju's voice broke through the fog. "If we could see where we are going, I would agree. As it is, I don't think we should turn our backs on an angry thundercloud."

"Quiet!" said Vakama. "Listen!"

The Toa Metru went silent. Now the air was filled with an ominous buzzing sound, which drew closer and closer. Not being able to see what caused it made it all the more frightening. "All right, keep calm," said Vakama. "Remember that we are Toa Metru, and we are together. As long as we stay united, we can overcome anything."

Privately, Vakama was not feeling quite so

confident. He thought he recognized that sound. If he was right, it came from a breed of Ta-Metru winged insects, nicknamed "fireflyers." Left alone, the small insects were relatively harmless. But when a swarm was angered, they would pursue an enemy halfway across the city.

Behind him, Matau had finally had enough. Bad enough to be wandering underground without all this danger and confusion. He raised his aero slicers and summoned a wind to blow the fog away. Although the best his weakened powers could manage was a stiff breeze, it was still enough to get the job done.

The fog dissipated, to reveal a sight out of every Matoran's nightmare: two powerful, menacing creatures, reptilianlike heads darting back and forth, staffs held tightly in their claws.

"Rahkshi!" shouted Whenua.

One of the Rahkshi was gold in color and now it screeched at the Toa. This Rahkshi had the ability to manipulate the weather within a limited range. Its partner, bright orange in color, was surrounded by a swarm of fireflyers. Controlled by the Rahkshi, the insects were just waiting for the signal to charge.

"What are they doing here?" asked Nokama.

"A better question is, what are we doing here?" said Onewa. "It took three squads of Vahki Zadakh to stop one Rahkshi that appeared in Po-Metru, and even then all they could do was drive the thing away."

"Then we will have to do better," said Nuju, blasting ice out of his crystal spikes. But his powers were not what they had been before the clash with the Morbuzakh, and the Rahkshi shrugged off the cold. The gold one hissed and unleashed a blizzard in the direction of the Toa.

Battered by wind and ice, the heroes fell back. Only Vakama saw the advantage they had gained — the intense cold was felling the fireflyers one by one. Angered, the orange Rahkshi was now advancing on the gold one.

Now the Toa were witness to a scene of complete chaos. The gold Rahkshi had summoned another storm and was hurling lightning bolt after lightning bolt at its insect-controlling cousin. What it did not realize was that a swarm of tiny devourers was pouring forth from every crack in the walls and floors. Devourers would consume any bit of inorganic protodermis they ran across. Rahkshi armor was definitely on their menu — and all of them were hungry.

"This would be really entertaining if we didn't have to get past them to go on," said Onewa. "Whenua, you're the librarian, what do you know about these things?"

The Toa of Earth had by now shaken off the lightning strike and regained his feet. "Rahkshi are very territorial and quick to anger. If we make a move toward them, they'll forget their own fight and turn on us again."

"But this isn't about us, is it?" said Nokama. "They have claimed this portion of tunnel as their own and they are defending it."

"Then that is the answer," said Nuju. "We make it not worth the effort to defend. Vakama, Whenua, I will need your help."

Nuju outlined his plan in as few words as possible. The Rahkshi's clash was becoming even wilder, threatening to bring the tunnel down around them. When the Toa of Ice nodded his head, Vakama placed his palms on the floor and sent waves of scorching heat through the stone. Meanwhile, Nuju used the remains of his elemental power to create icicles on the roof of the tunnel.

Just as the Rahkshi took notice of the heat underfoot, Whenua went to work with his earthshock drills. Driving them into the ground, he formed a crevasse that ran straight toward the Rahkshi. Both of the creatures had figured out the Toa were somehow responsible for the sudden change in conditions, and they were not happy about it.

Nuju's plan had worked halfway. The Rahkshi were definitely uncomfortable, but not rattled enough to flee from their chosen home. Vakama loaded a disk in his launcher and hurled it through the air at the gold Rahkshi. When it struck, the enlarging power invested in the disk caused the Rahkshi to shoot up rapidly, smashing its head into the ceiling and bringing icicles raining down.

The insect-controlling Rahkshi did not react as Vakama hoped. Instead of fleeing into the darkness of the tunnels, it charged forward toward the Toa. Nokama and Vakama reacted as one, he launching fire and she water at the oncoming creature. But when their energy streams collided, the result was a wall of steam. By the time the cloud cleared away, the Rahkshi was nowhere to be seen.

"Somehow I don't think a steam bath frightened it away," said Nuju. "It will be back."

"Mata Nui! Why don't you watch what you're doing?" Nokama snapped at the Toa of Fire. "I might have stopped it if you hadn't gotten in the way."

"I got in the way? That wasn't how it looked from here."

Nokama was about to say something else when she changed her mind. Arguing wasn't going to make anything better. "I'm sorry, Vakama. Neither of us was at fault. But this is exactly why I have been saying we need leadership. We cannot keep blundering through challenges without any strategy."

"Here's a strategy," said Onewa. "Let's stop talking and start moving, before we get any more surprises."

The Toa Metru resumed their journey into the tunnels. None of them noticed another pair of eyes watching them, eyes far more observant than any Rahkshi's could be. They noted the way each Toa moved and fought, filing the information away for later use. Then the owner of those eyes slipped away into the darkness without making a sound.

The hunt had begun.

The Toa Metru did not encounter any more difficulties as they penetrated the outer edges of the maintenance tunnels. Now and then a small Rahi would skitter across their path, only to vanish down a hole or among the pipes. As they moved deeper into the maze, the air grew increasingly stale. Matau wondered aloud how Onu-Matoran could stand to work down here.

"Practice," said Whenua. "Most Onu-Matoran start out as miners, digging for light-stones. You get used to the dark pretty quickly. If you're lucky, you get the opportunity to become an archivist, but even then you are indoors and underground much of the time. These tunnels might be a little extreme, but nothing an Onu-Matoran can't handle."

Onewa looked around. "I don't see any Ma-toran though."

"Well . . . see . . . some of the ones who have come down here in the past sort of . . . haven't come back."

"You said that was a legend," said Nokama.

"Evidently, Onu-Matoran legend has a basis in fact," muttered Nuju.

"Anything else you forgot to tell us, Whenua?" asked Onewa.

Whenua raised his lightstone to give the Toa Metru a good look at what lay ahead. "Just that."

The wide tunnel they were walking through came to an abrupt end at a stone wall a few paces away. Six narrow openings were visible in the wall, barely more than slits in the rock. "This is the start of the Fikou web," said Whenua. "From here, it's just narrow tunnels drilled into the rock, crisscrossing with each other, until we reach the main tunnel on the other side."

"Do we split up?" asked Vakama.

Whenua nodded. "The major crack in the seawall is on the other side of the web, but there could be damage closer to us as well. Each of us should take a tunnel. We'll see each other as we go, I'm sure, and then we can all meet up on the other side. Hang on to your lightstones. If you lose them, you might become a permanent resident down here."

"That's what I like about Onu-Matoran," said Matau. "They are always so full of happy-cheer."

Nokama chose the left-most tunnel. The passage was so narrow that it would have been impossible for two Toa to walk abreast. For one used to the freedom of the protodermis canals and the open sea, this space was far too cramped to be comfortable. She could well believe Matoran could go mad from too much time down here.

Not for the first time, she wondered if becoming a Toa Metru had been such a good thing. So far, she did not seem to get along very well with any of her comrades. They were certainly not the five she would have chosen as companions. Only Vakama had struck her as possessing real wisdom behind his shy front, and now she had fought with him, too. She knew he had it in him to be a leader. Why wouldn't he recognize it?

Nokama forced herself to get back to the job at hand. Using the lightstone, she examined every bit of the walls on either side, looking for cracks or leaks. One of these tunnels could flood in an instant, and while she could probably survive that, she wasn't so sure about the other Toa Metru. She hoped they were being careful.

The tunnel wound around and around like the body of a serpent. Smaller passages broke off to the left and right, usually dead-ending rapidly. Still, each of them had to be examined. She wondered how Whenua could even have considered doing this job on his own — it would have taken forever!

After a while, Nokama started to grow bored. One tunnel looked just like the other, and none of them showed any signs of damage. She wondered if this might be just a wild Rahi chase. Some Matoran thought he saw something, panicked, and ran for the nearest Toa. Back when she was teaching in Ga-Metru, she made a point of telling her students to always make sure of their facts before they spread a tale.

She rounded a corner, expecting to see the same dull stone walls she had seen a hundred times before. Instead, she froze at the sight of the orange Rahkshi standing in the middle of the corridor. Its armored head was open, but no sound came from the creature.

Nokama readied her hydro blades. The Rahkshi simply stared at her. Neither seemed to want to make the first move.

The Toa of Water considered her options. If she advanced, she would surely have to challenge the Rahkshi and might or might not win. If she retreated, the Rahkshi might see it as a sign of weakness and pursue.

While Nokama was making up her mind, the Rahkshi raised its staff and pointed it at her. A swarm of fireflyers appeared from the darkness and flew straight for her. Even as she braced for their stings, Nokama wondered why the

Rahkshi looked so surprised at the display of its own power. The creature was actually backing away, as if afraid of what it had unleashed.

Not that its sudden show of regret did anything to help the Toa of Water. The insects were already swarming around her, stinging and then flying away, only to return and sting again. Nokama's armored body was enough to blunt most of their stings, but enough got through to drive her to the ground. As soon as she was subdued, the fireflyers left, their orders fulfilled.

Only the Rahkshi remained, standing over the unconscious form of a Toa.

In another tunnel, Vakama was wrestling with his thoughts. Despite some of the things she had said, he felt sure Nokama was truly his friend. She even seemed to think he should be the leader of the Toa Metru. True, he had done a decent job at that during the confrontation with the Morbuzakh, but he wasn't at all sure he would want the role permanently.

I might look like a Toa . . . even act like one

sometimes . . . *but at heart, I am still a mask-maker,* he said to himself. His whole life had been spent working alone at his forge, crafting protodermis into Matoran masks and Masks of Power. It required patience, skill, and dedication, but it did not seem like the ideal job to prepare someone to lead Toa.

This has all happened too fast, he thought. *I went from being an average Matoran to suddenly having all these new powers and responsibilities. Others look at me differently, expect more from me.*

He paused to shine his lightstone on the wall. The rock was unmarred by any crack and looked like it had not changed in an eternity. *So why did I have to change?* he wondered. *Am I still Vakama? Or am I only the Toa of Fire now?*

He walked on, lost in thought. His eyes inspected the tunnel as he traveled, but his mind was back in Ta-Metru. For a moment, he wondered if it would ever be possible to go back to being a Matoran. But no, the legends said nothing about such a thing. A Toa was a Toa until he fulfilled his destiny, and then . . . what?

So caught up was he in his questions that at first he did not hear the footsteps ahead of him. When he finally did, he stopped . . . and so did they. When he resumed walking, the footsteps started again. Vakama wanted to call out and see if it was another Toa Metru, but then realized it might be a Rahkshi instead. No point in giving away his position if it wasn't necessary.

He moved forward cautiously. The Toa had been caught by surprise a few times too often since their transformation. He was determined that it would not happen again.

Disk launcher primed and ready, Vakama took a deep breath and charged around the bend in the tunnel. Yes, there was a figure up ahead. Lean, powerful, carrying some kind of wickedly sharp tools, it moved silently through the shadows. Then it stepped out into the light to reveal —

"Nokama?" Vakama looked at the Toa of Water, stunned. They had just parted a short time ago. Had her tunnel crisscrossed with his so quickly? "Have you spotted anything, or not?"

The Darkness Below

The Toa of Water shook her head slowly. "Not."

Vakama moved closer to her, only to see Nokama step back. "What's the matter? It's just me. No reason for you to be afraid."

"Not afraid," Nokama replied. "Have you spotted anything?"

"Well, some little Rahi, some cart tracks, and a few Matoran names scrawled on the walls," said Vakama. "Nothing I would worry about."

"Matoran," Nokama repeated quietly, almost as if it were a curse. "Well, I would worry."

Vakama walked up to Nokama. She looked troubled. "What is it? Did you —?"

The Toa of Fire stopped in mid-sentence. He was having another one of his visions, sudden flashes of the future like the one that had warned him about the Morbuzakh. He saw Toa Onewa lying on the ground, unconscious, and standing over him was . . . Vakama!

A blast of water shattered the vision into a thousand pieces as the Toa of Fire went flying down the tunnel. He crashed hard into the stone wall and hit the floor. Before he could gather his wits and get up again, Nokama had him pinned with the force of her water bursts. Even as his body struggled to get free, his mind struggled with questions. Why was she doing this? How had her elemental energies been restored to full power? Was Nokama planning to betray the other Toa Metru, and if so, for what purpose?

Vakama hoped to ask the Toa of Water these questions, if he was ever able to take another breath. But driven to the ground by the sheer, raw power of twin jets of water, it seemed more likely that he was about to become the first Toa to ever drown on dry land.

4

The gold Rahkshi moved carefully down the tunnel. Every one of its senses was on the alert. There were still intruders in its territory, and that was very bad. Intruders made loud noises and tried to drive the Rahkshi away, unless the Rahkshi struck first.

It could not hear the six from before, but it could smell them. They were no longer together and their scent carried traces of fear. That was pleasing to the Rahkshi. When the ones from up above carried fear into the tunnels, they were easier to find and easier to drive off.

The Rahkshi tried hard to remember how it had come to live in this place. But it could not. It had a vague memory of once living someplace else, then a long journey to the land above. But there were too many others there who tried to capture it. The Rahkshi escaped and fled down, down into the cold, welcoming dark.

The creature paused as it sensed another presence up ahead. Another Rahkshi, but not a threat. It stayed close to the wall as it moved forward until the other came into view. It was the orange Rahkshi from before, but now it was stretched out on the ground and not moving.

The gold Rahkshi crept closer. Why was the other so still? Was it hurt? Had the cold sleep overtaken it? No, the wormlike kraata inside was only stunned. Still, it wondered what could strike down a Rahkshi like this. Not one of the little ones from above. Not one of the six.

Wait! There was a scent in the air, strong and not unfamiliar to the Rahkshi. It had encountered a creature before with this scent, long ago when it first came to the tunnels. It sifted through dim memories trying to bring the image of the creature into focus.

Then suddenly the Rahkshi remembered it all. And with the memory came something else, something none of its kind had ever felt before . . .

Fear.

Onewa pulled himself painfully up to his hands and knees. He wasn't sure how long the world had been black, or exactly how he had wound up on the tunnel floor, unconscious.

The sight of scorch marks on the stone wall started bringing it all back to him. He had been exploring the tunnel when someone came up behind him. It was Vakama. The Toa of Fire seemed distracted, but he agreed to help Onewa check out some of the side passages. The Toa of Stone went back to work and then . . .

He did it! Onewa realized. *I felt the heat, and then the next thing I knew stalactites were falling down all around me.*

The Toa of Stone glanced up, already knowing what he would see. The stalactites had not broken off naturally — well-placed fire bursts had melted them free from the ceiling.

Onewa didn't know why a fellow Toa Metru would try to harm him, and he didn't really care. All that mattered was finding Vakama and showing him just what stone could do against fire.

In another tunnel not far away, Nokama too was awakening. She still ached from the fireflyer stings, but it was nothing she couldn't survive. No, she had something far more important to worry about.

In her mind, she went over every detail of her encounter with the insect-controlling Rahkshi. She recalled its every movement, its reaction to her, even the way its armored head had opened to allow the kraata inside to screech.

But it never made a sound, she realized. *When the armored plates opened . . . there was no kraata inside!*

Nokama was no Rahkshi expert. She had seen them in stasis tubes in the Archives, like any other Matoran, and one of them had run amok once in Ga-Metru before the Vahki brought it down. But she knew enough to be certain that a Rahkshi without its kraata was just an empty, if still frightening, suit of armor.

So that wasn't a Rahkshi, she thought grimly. *Not unless they grow them differently down here. I'd almost think I had imagined the whole thing, but the stings are real. It was something that* looked *like a Rahkshi, had the powers of one, and . . .*

Once, a long time before, Nokama and some of her friends had been playing near the canals on the border of Ga-Metru and Ko-Metru. Nokama had slipped and fallen in. The current had swept her into the other metru. The liquid protodermis had turned frigid when it traveled through Ko-Metru, and by the time she was rescued, she was half frozen. But that chill was nothing compared to what ran through her now.

If it can look like a Rahkshi, what else can it look like? she asked herself, already breaking into a run. *Or . . . who else?*

Vakama was furious.

He had awakened to find Nokama gone.

Apparently, the Toa of Water thought she had finished him off. He was on his way to prove her very wrong.

Toa Nuju had been walking for a very long time. At least, it seemed that way. As much as he disliked agreeing with Matau on anything, he was no more comfortable underground than was the Toa of Air. He missed the spires of Ko-Metru, the clean, crisp air, and most of all, the sight of the stars streaking by overhead. He belonged atop a Knowledge Tower, keeping watch over his metru, not wandering around Onu-Metru maintenance tunnels looking for leaks. Really, was this work for a Toa Metru?

Still, at least these narrow passages gave him an excuse to get away from the other Toa. If he had to listen to more arguing, or another one of Matau's bad jokes, he was going to freeze the whole lot of them. Maybe after they presented themselves to Turaga Dume at the Coliseum, he could go his own way and simply be the Toa of Ko-Metru.

His planning for the future was interrupted by a tremor that shook the entire tunnel network. This was followed by what sounded like a rock slide not far ahead. Images of the whole place coming down and trapping the six Toa Metru flashed through his mind. Nuju raced ahead, hoping he was wrong about what he had heard.

It was almost worse than he had expected. A whole portion of one of the walls had collapsed, and the glow from the lightstone revealed Matau half buried in stone. Nuju tried to freeze the rocks, with the idea of shattering them once frozen, but his power was too weak. Instead, he had to remove them one by one as he dug out the Toa of Air.

Matau revived just as Nuju finished. His eyes sparked to life and he hurled a mini-cyclone at Nuju. The Toa of Ice was blown back, but not hard enough to injure himself. "What was that for?" he demanded.

"Nuju? Is that you?" asked Matau.

"How many Toa of Ice do you think are

walking around down here?" Nuju said, giving Matau a hand up. "What happened to you?"

"Onewa," said Matau. "He's mad-crazy. I said hello and he brought the wall down on me."

"That doesn't sound like him," Nuju said, frowning. "You, maybe, but not him. Did you say anything to anger Onewa?"

Matau shook his head. "No. He waved and slide-down came the rocks. And look at this!"

The Toa of Air pointed to a spot high on the partially ruined wall. Nuju leaned in close and saw it was a burn mark. "He did that, too," insisted Matau. "Whoosh, hot-flame."

"All right. We had better find him," Nuju replied. "Before he finds someone else."

Nokama raced through the tunnels, fighting down her panic. A Rahkshi that wasn't a Rahkshi . . . what if Nuparu had not been Nuparu? What if all of this was an elaborate trap for the Toa Metru? Bring them down into the dark, separate them, and then . . .

No, she told herself. *Get ahold of yourself. Of course, Nuparu was really who he seemed to be. The crisis down here is real, but so is the danger if I don't find the other Toa Metru soon.*

Nokama's wish was granted in the next moment, as a fireball whizzed past her. It was too far away to be meant as anything but a warning, but it still made her ready her hydro blades. Her eyes struggled to pierce the darkness to find the source of the flame.

"This time you don't catch me by surprise." Vakama walked out of the shadows, disk launcher raised. "I don't know why you chose to turn on us, Nokama, but you'll never win."

"Wait! You don't understand!" Nokama shouted.

"You should have made sure I was defeated, Nokama," the Toa of Fire said as he launched a Kanoka disk at the Toa of Water.

Nokama didn't hesitate. She dove aside as the disk narrowly missed her. An instant later, it struck a stalagmite and shrunk it down to the size of a pebble. Nokama gasped.

"Vakama, don't make me defend myself," she cried. "Please listen to me!"

"I'll be glad to, once I know you're wrapped up tight," the Toa of Fire answered. He bent down and placed his palm on the stone floor. Nokama's eyes widened as the rock began to glow red, the wave of heat heading right for her.

"That . . . does . . . it!" Nokama said, launching herself into a flip. In midair, she hurled blasts of water at Vakama. Caught unawares, the Toa of Fire was swept off his feet and hit the ground hard. Nokama twisted her body and landed behind him.

But Vakama was ready for her. Guessing correctly where she would land, he rolled and came up launching another disk. This one found its target and Nokama felt an awful weakness overtake her. She dropped to her knees, barely able to hold her tools aloft.

The Toa of Fire got to his feet. "Stay down, Nokama. Please."

Nokama lifted her head and looked at Vakama. A horrible thought struck her: How could she know if this was really her friend? Maybe whatever impersonated the Rahkshi was after her again, this time in the form of someone she trusted. If that was the case, she couldn't afford to lose this struggle. Who knew what this . . . whatever it was . . . might be planning for the other Toa Metru?

Nokama struggled to draw on her elemental energies. If she could flood the tunnel, she could escape and warn the others. But she moved too slowly. Vakama had another disk ready, and was about to launch.

A sudden tremor rocked the tunnel. Rock rained down on the Toa of Fire, knocking him to the ground. Nokama looked past him to see the source: Onewa, eyes gleaming, proto pitons driven into the ground.

"Get away from her, Vakama," he snarled. "Time to put out your fire."

Nuju and Matau felt the tremor and immediately quickened their pace. "Do you have a thought-plan on what we do if Onewa's really turned bad?"

"We stop him," Nuju replied.

"No wonder you were a quick-smart scholar," Matau said, making no attempt to hide his sarcasm. "Then what? Give him to the Vahki? How will that make the rest of us Toa-heroes look?"

Matau had a good point. Nuju hated it when that happened. He could just picture show-ing up at the Coliseum to meet Turaga Dume, five Toa Metru with one tied up for delivery to the order enforcement squads. What kind of confidence would that inspire in the Matoran of Metru Nui? They would be finished before they even got started.

Another tremor shook the tunnels. "Let's worry about that when we capture him," said Nuju. "If we capture him."

Vakama was in the middle of a nightmare.

On one side, Nokama had recovered from her bout of weakness and was sending spheres of water in his direction. On the other, Onewa, apparently infected with the same madness she was, was bringing down half the tunnel. All the while, the Toa of Stone was ranting some nonsense about Vakama ambushing him.

Vakama still had no idea what was wrong with the two of them, but one thing was certain, he could not defeat two Toa Metru. It was all he could do to dodge Nokama's powers while melting the stone Onewa rained down on him. He wondered where Nuju, Matau, and Whenua were, or whether they had already fallen to their traitorous "friends."

There was no way Vakama could keep dodging forever without making a mistake. Moving to avoid flying rock, he placed himself in the path of one of Nokama's water bursts. The impact sent him to his knees. Onewa moved in for the capture.

"Maybe Turaga Dume will know how to heal whatever's wrong with you, fire-spitter," said the Toa of Stone. "Now I'll take the disk launcher."

Onewa reached for Vakama's Toa tool. But before he could grab it away, a sudden gust of wind lifted the Toa of Stone off his feet and hurled him down the tunnel. Vakama looked up to see Matau and Nuju standing nearby.

"Surprise," said the Toa of Air. "We followed your earth-shakers, Onewa, and got here everquick. Now why did you drop a wall on me?"

So I was right, Vakama thought. *Something* is *wrong with Onewa. Matau just proved it!*

Nokama rushed to help Onewa up and the two of them stood together. "You're wrong,

Matau. It's Vakama that has turned bad, not Onewa. You have to help us stop him."

"No! Onewa has tricked you," answered Matau.

"Something is very wrong here," Nuju said, just loud enough to catch everyone's attention. "Vakama took me by surprise, and Nokama says he did Onewa, too. But Matau says Onewa is the culprit . . . an Onewa who has the power of fire as well as stone."

"That's crazy!" snapped Onewa. "I haven't even seen Matau since we split up!"

"And Nokama challenged me," said Vakama. "This place must be driving us all mad."

"I suggest we stop fighting until we figure out the truth," said Nuju.

Slowly, reluctantly, the other Toa Metru accepted the wisdom of his words. They lowered their Toa tools and eyed one another warily. Onewa and Nokama stood on one side, Nuju and Matau on the other, and Vakama in the middle. But the voice that finally broke the uncomfortable silence did not belong to any of the five of them.

"About time," said Whenua, walking down the tunnel. "I thought I was going to have to wade into the middle of all of you."

The other Toa Metru all began talking at once, either warning Whenua or trying to explain how the conflict started. It was impossible to make out anything in the chaos of voices.

"Enough!" Whenua shouted. "You're all wrong. All of you were ambushed by another Toa Metru . . . and none of you were."

"What are you talking about?" demanded Onewa. "I know what happened to me."

Only Nokama seemed to understand. "Of course . . . the Rahkshi I saw —"

"Let me guess," said Whenua. "It looked like a Rahkshi, but something was off."

"Yes! How did you know?"

"It's called a Krahka, and I encountered it, too," the Toa of Earth explained. "A very dangerous Rahi. She defends herself by mimicking the appearance of an enemy, so well that she adapts their powers and abilities, too."

"That explains 'Onewa' using stone and fire powers at once. This Krahka must have adapted Vakama's powers and then his," said Nuju.

"But why is she after us? What did we do?" asked Nokama.

Whenua frowned. "This is her territory. We're intruders. Maybe she wants to drive us out."

"So what do we do? Run back up to Metru Nui because this thing wants us to?" said Onewa. "What about the Archives? What about the flooding?"

Whenua didn't have an answer for that. It was Vakama who finally said, "We stick together from now on. That way we can't be taken by surprise."

"That's quick-smart," said Matau. "And maybe we should hunt-track this Krahka before we worry about the leak."

"No!" said Whenua. "I think we need to get out now. You don't know what a Krahka is capable of."

The Toa Metru looked at one another. It

was Whenua's metru, and they had planned on letting him take the lead. But Toa running from anything, for any reason, felt wrong. Nuju put their feelings into words, saying, "Are we going to the Coliseum, then — or fleeing to it?"

Nokama looked at Vakama, thinking, *This is the time. Step up and be a leader. Make this decision.*

But Vakama didn't speak. Instead, it was Onewa who said, "No mindless Rahi is going to make me run. I say we go on, capture this thing, and then do what we set out to do here. Who's with me?"

One by one, all of the Toa Metru stepped forward. Whenua was the last to join the group. "All right, if we are going to do this," the Toa of Earth said, "then I better act as guide. I can take a guess where the Krahka might be hiding."

The six Toa Metru started walking through the tunnels, Whenua in the lead. Matau and Nuju trailed along behind, the Toa of Air looking puzzled.

"Nuju?"

"What?"

"If this Krahka can seem-look like anything it's seen . . . how will we know when we have found it?"

It was a very good question. Nuju wished he had a very good answer.

6

They had not been traveling for very long before most of the Toa Metru lost all track of where they were or how to get back. No one had thought to mark a trail as they proceeded through the tunnels. For his part, Whenua moved through the maze with complete confidence, never hesitating at any of the intersections.

So far, the journey had been without incident. The few small Rahi they had encountered ran from them. At one point, Vakama thought he spotted the gold Rahkshi, but it disappeared into the shadows before he could get a good look.

"Elementary translation," Nokama said softly.

Nuju turned to her. "What?"

"Elementary translation. That's what I would have been teaching today . . . if I had not become a Toa Metru."

"Do you regret the change?" asked the Toa of Ice.

Nokama shrugged. "No. No, of course not. We are heroes, aren't we? We can do things no one else can. But . . . when was the last time you saw a Toa playing a sport? Or jumping into chutes for the fun of it? Or doing any of the things Matoran do every day?"

Silence was Nuju's answer. His memory of Toa Lhikan was of a larger than life figure, defending the city against any threat and then returning, exhausted, to wait for the next call to action. He never seemed to have time for fun or friendship.

"I am not complaining about all we have gained," Nokama continued. "Just missing all we may have lost."

"Perhaps it is up to us to be a different kind of Toa Metru," said Nuju. "And to make sure that any Toa who follow us learn these lessons as well."

Whenua held up a hand. "Stop. Look ahead."

The floor of the tunnel before them had

collapsed, evidently long ago. A flimsy bridge made from Le-Metru cable had been constructed over the chasm. It was the right width and strength for a party of Matoran crossing, but looked far too weak to support six Toa Metru.

"Is there another way across?" asked Nokama.

Whenua shook his head.

"Then we go this way, earth-digger," said Onewa. "One at a time."

The bridge consisted of a single cable, attached to two others higher up that served as handrails. Whenua stepped carefully onto the cable and began to quickly make his way across. When he was halfway across the span, the darkness below the bridge began to move.

"Mata Nui protect us . . . what is that?" said Nokama.

Nuju peered over the edge. "Stone rats. Thousands of them."

"Hundreds of thousands," said Vakama. "Their warrens must have been disturbed when the tunnel collapsed."

"Dangerous?" asked Matau.

"You wouldn't want one for a pet," Onewa replied. "Their teeth are made for eating through solid rock. Put an Ussal cart or a chute, or even a Knowledge Tower, between them and dinner and they'll eat that, too."

Whenua kept moving as if he hadn't even noticed the creatures below. He reached the other side and beckoned the others to follow. Nokama took a step onto the bridge and paused, seeing the thousands of red eyes down below and hearing the chittering of hungry stone rats.

"How come the Chronicles never talk about things like this?" she said.

"Probably because the Chronicler ran away," Onewa chuckled. "Only Toa are brave enough for this kind of work."

"Brave enough, or foolish enough?"

"Brave, if we make it across," the Toa of Stone answered. "Foolish, if we don't."

Nokama closed her eyes and focused all her concentration within. Ga-Metru Matoran were trained in both mental and physical disciplines, for the two went hand in hand. She struggled to remember all that she had learned about maintaining perfect balance. When she finally felt ready, the Toa of Water opened her eyes and started across the bridge.

As she walked, slowly and steadily, nothing existed for her except the cable beneath her feet. There were no rats below, no Toa behind, no sights or sounds that were not directly related to her task. She was not even aware that she had made it to the other side until Whenua grabbed her hand to steady her for the last few steps.

"Well, if she can do it . . ." said Matau. Then he sprang into the air, flipped over, and grabbed both hand cables. As the other Toa watched in shock, he proceeded to cross the bridge by walking on his hands. "This is the way a Toa-hero does it!"

"That's the way an Ussal driver who's gone round one chute too many does it," muttered Onewa. "Vakama, you're next."

If the Toa of Fire was fearful, he didn't show it. Disk launcher at the ready, he walked as swiftly as he could across the cable. He had almost reached the end when he heard Nokama shout his name.

Vakama whirled to see a ghostly figure rising from out the sea of stone rats. At first its identity wasn't clear. But as it passed through the bridge to hover in the air, he could see it was a Rahkshi with a black head and spine, and dark green claws and feet. Vakama launched a disk at the floating creature, only to see it pass right through the target.

"Nothing to fear-worry about," said Matau. "If you can't touch it, then it can't touch you, right?"

The Rahkshi screeched in answer. Then before the Toa's startled eyes, it went from ghostly to solid and plunged down. The creature struck the bridge, tearing one end loose. Vakama grabbed the cable and hung on as he slammed into the rock wall.

Down below, the stone rats scrambled in anticipation of the Rahkshi falling toward them. At the last moment, the creature's density changed once more and it floated upward again.

Frustrated, a few of the stone rats turned to the end of the cable bridge now resting in their midst. Cautiously at first, they began to climb the cable. Seeing their success, more began to follow, crawling toward Vakama.

The Toa of Fire climbed hand over hand toward the ledge. Nokama held out her hydro blade for him to grab on to. "Hurry! They're coming!"

Vakama looked down. The stone rats were now racing up the cable. In moments, they would be upon him and then up onto the ledge where Nokama, Matau, and Whenua stood. He could tell he would not make it all the way up in time. There was only one thing left to do.

Grabbing a disk, Vakama slammed it into the cable. The weakness power in the Kanoka disk combined with the sharp edge of the disk itself to sever the line. Toa of Fire, bridge, and stone rats fell together toward the chasm far below.

"Vakama!" Nokama screamed.

Onewa and Nuju watched helplessly as their friend plummeted down. "Ice?"

"I tried," said Nuju. "My elemental powers are exhausted!"

Matau pushed past Nokama. "Not losing a Toa-friend today!" Before she could stop him, he dove off the ledge.

Vakama saw the Toa of Air plunging toward him. Matau was shouting, "Slow yourself! Flip over, Vakama!"

The Toa of Fire had no idea what Matau was planning, but he wasn't going to argue. Letting go of the cable, Vakama executed a series of midair flips to slow his fall. As he completed the third one, he felt Matau grab his wrists.

"Now we go high-flying!" shouted Matau.

A sudden gust of wind lifted both Toa toward the ceiling. Vakama glanced below to see the cable bridge disappearing beneath the swarm of stone rats.

"Beats ground-walking now, doesn't it?" laughed Matau.

"Sure. Unless you fly right into a Rahkshi. Watch out!"

Matau turned to see the Rahkshi hovering right in his path. Unable to shift the winds in time to change their course, he and Vakama plunged right through the misty substance of the creature. Then the Rahkshi suddenly solidified and grabbed on to Vakama's leg. Toa Metru and Rahkshi dropped like a stone.

"Matau! We need a stronger wind!" shouted Vakama.

"Or one less wind-rider!" snapped Matau.

The Toa of Fire tried to shake off the Rahkshi, but the creature wasn't letting go. He mustered the strongest flame he could, but the Rahkshi simply turned insubstantial and let the fire go right through it before resuming its grip on Vakama.

"It's not letting go!"

"It will, Toa-brother," replied Matau. "I don't think it will like where we're going!"

The Toa of Air summoned all his strength and channeled it into a powerful wind that flung the three of them on a collision course with the rock wall. Vakama glanced up to see complete determination in Matau's eyes. He never wavered as he steered them directly toward a final crash.

Great, thought Vakama. *Never thought my last moments would be spent with a deranged Toa who thinks he's a Gukko bird.*

The Toa of Fire was tempted to close his eyes as the wall grew closer and closer. But he did not. Toa Lhikan would have met his end with eyes open and head held high, and Vakama would not shame that tradition by showing fear.

An instant before a certain, shattering impact, Matau suddenly swerved upward, taking Vakama with him. The Rahkshi was whipped hard toward the wall and instinctively turned intangible to avoid the crash. Its hands slipped right through Vakama's ankle and it sailed off, passing through the rock and disappearing into the wall.

Matau winced at the sight. "Hope that Rahkshi doesn't think to go solid while it's in there."

Suddenly, the Toa dropped, rose, and then dropped again. "What's going on?" asked Vakama.

"My power is fading!" answered Matau. "The winds won't close-listen anymore!"

The Toa of Air fought to stay aloft. More than once, it looked as if they were going to become much better acquainted with the stone rats than either Toa wanted to. Finally, Matau managed to steer them above the ledge where Nokama and Whenua waited. That was when his power at last gave out completely, sending them both toward the stone floor.

Nokama moved quickly to catch Vakama. But Matau fell hard right in front of Whenua, who did not act in time to prevent it. "Thanks for the quick-save," the Toa of Air grumbled. "Next time, you can rescue the fire-spitter and I will stay safe on the ledge."

"What you did was very brave," Nokama said to Matau. "But you shouldn't have had to do it." She turned to Vakama. "We could have handled the stone rats, if it came to that, Vakama. You didn't have to sacrifice yourself."

There was no anger in her words, but they stung just the same. Worse, Vakama knew she was right. They were all Toa Metru now. By acting like he had to protect the others, he had only succeeded in placing his and Matau's lives at risk.

Will I ever be done learning how to be a Toa? he wondered. *The lessons keep getting harder. Fail one and you may not get a chance to try another.*

"I wish I could say all is well, but we still have a problem," said Nokama, gesturing across the chasm. "Make that three. Two Toa Metru on the other side, and no bridge. So . . . whose turn is it to come up with the great idea?"

Watching from the other side, Onewa shook his head. "If we wait for that group to save us, we will end up Rahi bones here. What do you say we take a leap into the future, Nuju?"

Before the Toa of Ice could respond, Onewa had grabbed him by the arm and jumped off the ledge. His powerful legs propelled them well out over the chasm, but nowhere near far enough to reach the other Toa. It looked as if the stone rats were about to receive two unexpected gifts.

Onewa did not look at all worried. As the

two Toa reached the apex of their leap, he used his Toa power on the ground far below. An instant later, a pillar of stone shot up midway across the span and directly in the path of the Toa of Stone.

Casting one of his proto pitons ahead of him, Onewa caught the pillar with it and swung to relative safety, Nuju in tow. The Toa of Ice looked at him and said coldly, "Don't . . . *ever* . . . do . . . that . . . again."

"Relax, scholar," replied Onewa. "You'll get used to it."

With a yell, Onewa launched the two of them into the air again. The other Toa Metru scattered just in time as they landed on the ledge, Onewa tucking and rolling to minimize the impact and Nuju crashing hard into the rock.

The Toa of Stone was the first to reach his feet, in time to see Nuju rise and charge toward him. Vakama moved quickly to keep the two apart. "If my powers were at their peak, hammer-swinger, no one would be hearing from you until the thaw," growled Nuju.

"Big talk from a stargazer," snapped Onewa. "Try doing real work sometime."

"Hold it!" said Vakama. "Both of you. We have done enough fighting among ourselves."

"This is no way for Toa Metru to behave," said Nokama. "What would Turaga Dume say if he saw this?"

"Turaga Dume will never get the chance to anger-speak or anything else to us if we don't get moving," said Matau. "Save the shout-loud for when we are out of this place."

"Yes, let us keep going. We are almost at the end," said Whenua, frowning. Without waiting for an answer from his friends, he turned and started walking farther into the tunnels.

Matau watched him go and shook his head. "If he gets any more dark and grim, I will call him Toa of Mud."

Nokama said nothing. But her eyes never left Whenua as the team resumed its journey.

7

The Toa of Stone caught up to Whenua sometime later. "Any plan for what we do when we find this thing?"

"No," Whenua answered.

"Ever had to get a shape-shifter like this into the Archives before?"

The Toa of Earth seemed to puzzle over that question for a long time, before he finally said, "How would we know if we had?"

The path narrowed, and then widened again. Although their lightstones were still working well, the gloom seemed heavier here and the shadows harder to drive away. Eventually, despite the bright glow of the stones, the darkness became impossible to pierce and the Toa Metru were forced to halt.

"This cannot be natural," said Nokama quietly. "This blackness feels almost . . . alive."

"I think you are imagining things," said Nuju. "Darkness is just the absence of light. It cannot be a living thing."

"Let's keep going," said Onewa. "Follow my voice, this way. No, wait, I think that's the way we came. Maybe we had better go the other way. I —"

The Toa of Stone's voice cut off abruptly. Nokama called his name, but he did not answer. The other Toa Metru stood perfectly still, but could not hear their friend — or anything else — moving.

Finally, Whenua said, "This way," and the others moved toward the sound. They walked single file, the Toa of Earth in the lead, followed by Nokama, Nuju, Matau, and Vakama. If Onewa was trailing along behind, he gave no sign. Every now and then, one of the Toa would glance over their shoulder, but no one could see anything through the shadows.

Vakama was troubled. Onewa might not be the easiest Toa to work with, but he was no coward. He wouldn't have just run off and abandoned his friends.

Something happened to him, and if we're not careful, the same thing will happen to us, he said to himself.

Even as the words raced through Vakama's mind, something snaked through the darkness to wrap around his legs, arms, and mask. For a moment, he thought perhaps the Morbuzakh vines had returned, but this felt different. Then lack of air cut off his thoughts and he blacked out. The mysterious thing that had grabbed Vakama now dragged him away.

"Vakama, perhaps your fire could brighten the way," Nokama said. "Do you have enough power left to try?"

But the Toa of Fire did not answer. Nokama stopped short, and Nuju walked into her. "Why are you stopping?" asked the Toa of Ice.

"I think Vakama is gone, too!" she answered. "Something is in this darkness with us, Nuju. How do we fight what we can't see?"

She reached out to find Nuju. But her hand

instead encountered what felt like an energy field. A tingle ran up her arm and she pulled back violently as her limb began to grow dead. "Nuju! I felt something!"

When Nokama extended her arm a second time, the field was gone . . . and so was the Toa of Ice.

"Whenua! Matau! Are you there?"

"Ground-walking right behind you," said Matau. "What's happened to the others?"

"They found side passages?" suggested Whenua.

Nokama was surprised that the Toa of Earth did not sound more concerned. But then he knew better than any of them how easy it was to get lost down here.

"I think we should link hands," Nokama said.

"Great idea!" Matau replied. "But maybe Whenua should scout ahead, and we two can stay hand-linked back here."

"Very funny, Matau."

Nokama took hold of Whenua's hand. But when she reached for Matau's, the Toa of Air was gone. It took every bit of her willpower not to panic. If the other Toa were in danger, only she and Whenua were left to save them.

Now Whenua was tugging her forward so hard that she almost left her feet. The darkness was breaking up around her now and she could see flashes of stone walls. The next moment, the oppressive shadow was gone completely and Nokama blinked as she adjusted to the sudden light.

She and Whenua were standing in a cavern, alone. There was no sign of the other Toa or what had taken them. The Toa of Earth looked around and said, "I warned them this would be dangerous. We should have turned back."

"It's too late for that now," snapped Nokama. "We have to find them. I'm not leaving these tunnels without the others."

"Well, that's half right," muttered Whenua. "Going back will just get us trapped. We should go forward. If they are lost . . . I doubt they will ever be found."

Nokama whirled to look at the Toa of Earth. Whenua had made those comments as if he were talking about a misplaced tool. "You're right, Whenua. It is very dangerous down here, isn't it? But the Toa of Earth volunteered to guide us through the tunnels of his metru. That way, we could avoid the most perilous spots — or could we?"

She crossed her hydro blades in front of her and took a step back, now battle ready. "The six Toa Metru could triumph over any foe. But if one of us was *not* one of us, treachery would win the day. That is what you counted on, wasn't it, Krahka?"

Before Nokama's eyes, "Whenua" morphed into the exact image of Vakama. "I wondered when you would figure it out, Toa. You would not leave my domain, even when one of your own suggested it . . . and now you will never leave."

"So some of what you said was the truth," Nokama answered. "You can look like any one of us. And you were the Rahkshi I encountered, weren't you?"

Another shift and now Nokama was facing the yellow Rahkshi. Then she turned back to

Vakama. "Yes. No real Rahkshi would be fooled, but their senses are more acute than yours."

"Why go to all this trouble?" Nokama said, circling to get the best defensive position. "Why not just appear as Turaga Dume and order us out of the tunnels?"

"I can only take the form of those I have encountered," said the Krahka, quickly shape-shifting from Vakama to Nuju to Onewa. "And it took me time to learn your language. When I first met Vakama, in your shape, I could only re-peat back words he had said to me."

Now the Krahka cycled through all six Toa Metru, ending up as Whenua again. "Now I have learned. I have adapted. It is too late for all of you."

"Where's the real Whenua? What have you done to him?"

"No more than I did to the rest of the Toa," the Krahka said in Whenua's booming voice. "These tunnels are a haven for Rahkshi. Rahkshi who can coil their elastic bodies around you . . . or teleport you away . . . or trap you in a stasis field . . . or simply cloak you in silence so no one can hear you scream."

Nokama kept moving, staying out of reach of the Krahka. She knew that the longer the Rahi talked, the more time her elemental powers would have to strengthen. "Why not just let us leave? We mean no harm to you."

For just a split second, the Krahka took on the hideous form of a half Rahkshi, half Toa. Then she changed to Matau. "Because you would not leave. Top-dwellers never do. But this is my place. Here you are the invaders. You are not welcome."

Nokama started to reply, then stopped short. The Krahka's words could have just as easily been said by the Toa to the Morbuzakh plant when it threatened Metru Nui. Was this creature really doing nothing more than defending her home? Still, Nokama had to save her friends. If the Krahka was determined to get in the way, then a clash was inevitable.

"You realize if we don't return, more 'top-dwellers' will come down here," said the Toa of

Water. "They will search for us. Your home will be torn apart. Is that really what you want?"

"If they search for you, they will find you," said the Krahka, shifting to Vakama's form. Then in the voice of the Toa of Fire, she said, "The Toa Metru have discovered a danger to the city lurking far underground. We are going to stay here until the danger is ended."

Nokama's mind reeled. She had never even considered . . . but it made sense. The Krahka could fool everyone into thinking the Toa safe and on a mission. For that matter, other than Nuparu, who even knew they were down here? Who would go looking for them?

Three shapes emerged from the tunnels and into the cave. They were Rahkshi, one silver, one black-white, one tan-blue. "I sensed great power in you, Nokama, more than you realize," said the Krahka. "It is a shame you will never live up to your potential."

Vakama/Krahka slipped away as the three Rahkshi moved in. They seemed to shy away from the Krahka, perhaps disturbed by the conflict between what they scented and what they saw. But they had no such reluctance about pursuing Nokama.

The three spread out, surrounding Nokama. She feinted right and then dove for the legs of the tan-blue Rahkshi. But when she reached the spot, the creature faded away as if it had never been there. Then it reappeared a short distance away.

Teleportation? Nokama wondered as she scrambled to her feet. *No . . . illusion. I see it where it's not.*

She did not have much time to think about that. The silver Rahkshi hurled a lightning bolt in her direction. She managed to dodge the full impact, but enough of the energy brushed her that she was thrown across the room. Nokama never struck the ground, though. Instead, she found herself whirled about in a cyclone created by the black-white Rahkshi.

When the winds abruptly died down, Nokama landed hard on the cavern floor. Staggering, she had to make a real effort to draw herself up to her hands and knees. The three Rahkshi stood their ground, not coming close enough for her to grab. She tried to stand up, but a jagged bolt of lightning just above her head killed that idea.

Strangely enough, the Rahkshi's actions made her feel less fearful. If they had been convinced they could defeat her, they would have closed in already. Instead, they maintained their distance and tried to keep her off balance.

They don't know what to make of me, she realized. *Maybe they have never seen a Toa before. That means they have no idea how powerful I might be.*

"I appreciate the rest. All that walking was tiring," she said, trying to sound confident. "You do not believe a mere three of you can stop a Toa, though, do you?"

The Rahkshi stirred. They didn't understand the words, but they sensed that the tone was not that of a defeated foe. Nokama was trying to decide what to do next when she heard a welcome sound — the dripping of liquid protodermis through a minute crack in the wall. The leak was only a short distance away, to her left, but the black-white Rahkshi was between her and the slowly forming puddle.

Just where I want him, she thought.

"Compared to what I just faced up above, you three aren't even worth wasting my Toa power on. Oh, maybe you scare all the little Rahi that skitter around down here, but up above we laugh at things like you," she continued.

Nokama kept talking to distract the Rahkshi from what she was really doing — extending her power to draw a stream of liquid protodermis from the site of the leak right to her. Conveniently, the stream passed right beneath the feet of the black-white Rahkshi.

"Actually, you are fortunate to have run into me," she said, mockingly. "Vakama or Nuju, they might really hurt you."

The thin line of liquid had almost reached her. The black-white Rahkshi's attention was focused on her. It had never noticed what she had done. Now it was time to see if her plan was going to work.

She locked her gaze on the silver Rahkshi and snarled, "I have had enough of this. Get out of my way." Then she lunged forward as if about to spring.

The Rahkshi reacted with a bolt of chain lightning, but Nokama wasn't sitting and waiting for it. Instead of springing, she rolled to her left. The bolt struck where she had been, hitting the stream of protodermis and traveling along it right back to the black-white Rahkshi. The current slammed into the creature and sent him flying.

Nokama swung her hydro blades hard and cleaved open the wall at the site of the leak. Liquid protodermis gushed through the gap, rapidly filling the cave. Both Rahkshi's faceplates opened to reveal very disturbed kraata, screeching their rage.

Then she noticed an unexpected benefit of the flood. The liquid was disturbed a few feet to the right of the tan-blue Rahkshi. That was where the true creature stood, well away from the illusion. She mustered her energy and sent a mini-tidal wave toward the spot. When it struck, the illusion vanished and the real Rahkshi appeared, knocked off its feet.

One out of the fight, one stunned, she said to herself. *And one to go.*

She had half hoped the silver Rahkshi would back off. But if anything, all she had succeeded in doing was making it angry. Wary, too — having seen what happened to its brother, it wasn't going to be hurling any more lightning bolts around. Still, it advanced toward Nokama through the waist-deep liquid, claws outstretched.

The Toa of Water nodded. She knew the best she could hope for was to slow down these creatures and buy time for escape. So far, she had been lucky. But now the silver Rahkshi had taken her measure and was prepared for her moves. *All but one,* she reminded herself.

Without warning, she dove beneath the surface of the protodermis and rocketed toward the Rahkshi. At the last moment, she veered off and began circling it at enormous speed. By the time the creature grasped what was happening, it was too late. The Rahkshi was caught inside a powerful waterspout, heading for the ceiling.

Nokama kept swimming, faster and faster, until she heard the sharp crack of Rahkshi armor striking stone high above. Then she abruptly stopped and let the spout dissipate. The Rahkshi crashed into the liquid and then floated to the surface, lying on its back. Its faceplate was open and the leechlike kraata inside was trying to squirm out.

Nokama decided there would never be a better time to leave.

8

She found Vakama, Matau, and Onewa fairly easily. All three were unconscious but unharmed, tucked away in alcoves until the Rahkshi decided just what to do with them. Nuju was more of a problem. The Toa of Ice was surrounded by some kind of energy field that could not be pierced. His heartlight flashed and his eyes were open, but he seemed unaware of what was going on.

"You know, I think I like him better this way," Onewa commented.

"Yes, but do you want to lift-carry him everywhere?" asked Matau. "I don't."

Vakama tried again to reach inside the field. This time, the resulting jolt was so violent he dropped his disk launcher. Onewa bent to pick it up.

"Here, fire-spitter. I know you would be lost without it," the Toa of Stone said.

Matau smiled, but the expression quickly faded, replaced by a look of excitement. He rushed to where the other two Toa Metru were standing. "The launcher! That is the puzzle-answer!"

Onewa looked at Matau as if the Toa of Air had lost his mind, especially when he started sifting through Vakama's disks searching for just the right one. Suddenly, he held one high and said, "Aha! Found it!"

Matau had grabbed a teleportation disk. The Toa of Fire was beginning to get an idea of what his friend had in mind, and decided Onewa was probably right: he was crazy.

"See? Nuju is inside the field, but not part of it. So if you quick-launch a teleportation disk at the field . . ."

"And if you're wrong, we send Nuju to Mata Nui only knows where," Onewa said. "It's too dangerous."

Vakama took the disk from Matau. "But we're going to do it," he said, loading it into the launcher. "We have no choice. The only alternatives are leave him here, or hope to track down whatever did this to him and get them to undo it."

"Easy for you to say, mask-maker," grumbled Onewa. "You're not the one stuck inside that thing."

"If Matau's plan fails, Nuju is no worse off than he is now," Nokama interjected. "He is just no worse off someplace else."

Vakama raised the launcher. "Stand aside, Onewa."

"Listen, you can't tell me —"

Nokama laid a hand on Onewa's arm and gently guided him off to the side. "Please. Every moment we delay here could mean greater danger for Whenua."

Vakama took a deep breath. Hitting the target would be easy, but there was no telling what effect the disk would have. If Nuju vanished along with the field, they might never see him again. *But he always says we don't worry enough about consequences anyway. Now we will see if he's right,* Vakama said to himself.

The disk flew from the launcher and struck

the energy field. There was a bright flash, blinding for the Toa who had spent so much time in near darkness. Then Matau hurried forward to catch a collapsing Nuju.

"It worked!" the Toa of Air shouted. "Meet the wisest of all Toa-heroes!"

"Is Nuju all right?" asked Nokama. "Is he hurt?"

The Toa of Ice looked around at the other Toa Metru. Then he said, "Why are we standing around here? We need to find the Krahka so we can get out of this foul pit. Why any Matoran would want to spend time underground is beyond me."

"He's healthy-fine!" announced Matau.

Nokama led the way deeper into the tunnels. She was operating purely on instinct. There was no logical reason to believe Whenua was not somewhere back in the tunnel maze, unconscious or worse. But something told her the Krahka would not have left him there for the Toa to find.

If I'm right, by the time the Krahka encoun-

tered Whenua, she knew the true power of the Toa, Nokama told herself. *And she knew the Rahkshi might not be able to defeat us. I think Whenua is her protection against us.*

None of which made it any easier to guess which path the Krahka took. Faced with multiple choices, Nokama went with whichever tunnel was the narrowest and most treacherous. It only made sense, given that nothing else on this journey had been easy.

Eventually, one of the Toa had to ask the question. It was Onewa who finally spoke up. "Nokama, do you have any idea where we're going?"

"No. I don't know these tunnels, so I am guessing. I'm not Whenua."

"That's all right," Matau said. "After all, it turned out Whenua wasn't Whenua either."

"Does anyone else feel warm?" Nuju asked.

Vakama reached up and touched one of the pipes that ran overhead. It was broiling hot. "We may be under Ta-Metru. That is molten pro-todermis in those pipes. So be careful — not even our Toa armor would protect us from the heat."

"Is there anything else we need to worry about?" asked Onewa.

Vakama gestured at a half dozen long, black shapes uncoiling from the pipes. "Oh, just those."

Nokama jumped back so fast she slammed into Matau behind her. "*What* . . . are those?"

One of the serpentlike creatures hit the ground. The stone sizzled and steamed underneath it. "We call them lava eels," said Vakama. "Sometimes Matoran find small ones near the forges and bring them home. Then they get too big and destructive, so they get abandoned. Some lurk around the furnaces, some hide in the reclamation yards . . . and some wind up here."

"How destructive is destructive?" asked Nuju.

Vakama bent down and tossed a handful of pebbles at one of the eels. No sooner had the small stones struck than they were reduced to ash.

"I would guess their owners don't pet them very much," said the Toa of Ice.

The lava eels drew closer and began to spread out. They left scorch marks everywhere they slithered. More eels appeared behind the Toa, apparently just as curious about their visitors. In a matter of moments, the heroes were surrounded.

"Is this bad?" asked Nokama. "If so, how bad?"

Vakama shook his head. "We are fine as long as we move slowly. Lava eels are not by nature hostile creatures. As long as nothing agitates them, we'll be able to —"

The rest of the Toa of Fire's sentence was cut off by a roar that shook the tunnel. It was impossible to tell just where it came from, but its effects were obvious. The eels began to hiss and squirm, their bodies heating up rapidly. Almost too late, Onewa saw what was about to happen.

"Jump!"

All five Toa Metru leaped and grabbed on to the pipes as the tunnel floor dropped away beneath them. Some weren't so sure they had gained anything with the move, since the searing heat of the pipes made it nearly impossible to hang on.

"They melted right through the stone!" Onewa said, looking down into the dark pit that yawned below his feet. "Whatever made that roar scared them."

The roar came again, so loud it rattled the pipes and sent the eels slithering for cover. Now the Toa could see it came from a huge, dark shape that was pacing at the bottom of the pit. "I think we just seek-found 'whatever' — any idea what that is?" asked Matau.

"I didn't think anything lived beneath the maintenance tunnels," Nokama said.

The shadowy beast gave out another roar. "Maybe we just found the reason why that's so," Onewa replied. "Unless we want to get a closer look at our friend, we better move."

One by one, the Toa began to swing back and forth on the pipes. Every move was agonizing as they clung to the boiling pipes. When they had built up enough momentum in their swings, they let go and sailed over the pit and onto the stone floor beyond. Their landings were neither soft nor gentle, but what mattered was being far from protodermis pipes and massive, angry Rahi.

"Is everyone all right?" asked Vakama.

"Battered. Burned. Bruised," reported Matau, smiling. "So what's our next Toa-hero deed?"

"Sometimes I think you like this job a little too much," grumbled Onewa.

Matau laughed. "We quick-save Matoran. We defeat evil. We get to explore ever-strange places like this. A little discomfort is not so very bad compared to that."

Nokama smiled and shook her head. There were times it seemed that Matau might not be the brightest lightstone in the tunnel, and then he would come out and say just the right thing. He was correct, of course. For all the trouble and the danger, they were all having adventures they would never forget.

Someday, we will look back on these times with wonder, she thought. *We will share our tales, and all of Metru Nui will be amazed at what once went on here. I wonder how they will look at us? Will they even remember the Toa Metru?*

Vakama's voice interrupted her thoughts. "Nokama, we have to keep moving. Whenua is depending on us."

Yes, thought Nokama as she rose. *Time to write another tale of the Toa.*

Nuju volunteered to scout ahead. Nokama and Matau felt it better if all the Toa Metru stayed together, but he needed time to himself. There had been few spare moments to contemplate all the recent changes. The realization that he would no longer be a Ko-Metru seer, but instead the guardian of the entire metru, was . . . disturbing. Somehow, he had thought that once the Morbuzakh was defeated, he and the others would become Matoran again.

Now, of course, he could see that was not so. Toa were Toa as long as they needed to be to fulfill their destiny. He wondered if he would ever get the chance for quiet study again, or if his life would now be nothing but twisted plants, giant Rahi, and rescuing Whenua.

He slowed his pace as he neared a bend in the tunnel. Light was spilling out from somewhere up ahead, in a place where no light should be. He edged closer to the corner and stole a look ahead.

The chamber beyond was large and dominated by a huge pit in the center filled with bubbling, molten protodermis. No one seemed to be in the cave, other than the occasional Rahkshi that would wander through and then leave in a hurry. Nuju guessed there must be a rear exit, probably another tunnel.

He waited until the cave was completely empty before sneaking closer. From the cave mouth, it did not look any different. Lightstones were mounted around the chamber, but there did not seem to be any other signs of habitation. *Maybe something lived here, and left,* he thought.

"Nuju! Up here!"

Startled, the Toa of Ice looked up. There was Whenua, pasted to the ceiling above the pit by some sort of webbing. He was bound so tightly that only his head could move. "Is it really you?" he asked.

"Of course it's —" Nuju began sharply. Then he remembered what it was the Toa Metru were challenging. When he spoke again, his tone was more gentle. "Yes, Whenua, it's really me. The others are not far behind Are you all right?"

"I have been hanging here trying to re-member if a Toa ever met his end by being baked while stuck to a ceiling," Whenua replied. "I can't think of one. As an archivist, I am excited about discovering a first. As a Toa Metru, I am not look-ing forward to being remembered in the Chron-icles for this."

"You won't be. We'll find some way to get you down from there. But what happened to you?"

"The Krahka, posing as Onewa, took me by surprise," said Whenua. "When I woke up, she had turned into something else — something awful — and I was bound like this. Where did you say the others were?"

"We are here," Nokama said, surveying the

scene from the cave mouth. "We have little time. Nuju, guard the other exit."

The Toa of Ice turned to do as Nokama had asked. Too late, Whenua shouted a warning. Too late, Nuju turned to see that "Nokama" was now "Onewa" and stone was erupting from the cave floor to envelop him. In an instant Nuju was trapped in a cocoon of rock.

"You Toa are so trusting," the Krahka hissed. "One day, it will be the death of you."

9

Nokama was growing concerned. Nuju had been gone for a long time, without so much as a word back to the others about what he had found. With the number of unexpected dangers down here, the Toa of Ice might be in just as much trouble as Whenua.

Then again, he may simply be happier on his own, she reminded herself. Ko-Matoran have never liked crowds.

Vakama saw Nokama's demeanor and guessed what was bothering her. It was disturbing him, as well, but for different reasons. "Nuju?" he asked.

"Yes. We should never have let him go off alone. We should have insisted all of us stay together."

"Do you think he would have listened if we

had?" said Vakama. "Besides, he will be back. I know he will. And we have to be prepared."

"What are you talking about?" asked Nokama.

"Get Onewa and Matau. We have a great deal to discuss, and not much time."

As Vakama predicted, it did not take long for Nuju to reappear. "I thought you would have made more progress by now," he said.

"We were waiting to hear from you," Vakama replied. "What did you find?"

"Nothing but more and more tunnels. I thought I saw light at one point down a side branch, but then it disappeared. Probably just some glowing Rahi."

"Probably. Well, we have decided to stop here for a while until help arrives."

"Help?" asked Nuju. "What help? And where is Matau?"

Nokama shook her head. "We realized while you were gone that this place is simply too big for us to search. We will never find Whenua this way. So Matau volunteered to go back to the surface and bring back six squads of Vahki. They will take the tunnels apart, stone by stone. You know nothing can hide from them."

"No, of course not," Nuju said softly. "How long ago did he leave?"

"Not long," said Onewa. "But he travels fast."

Nuju turned and started to walk away. Vakama put a hand on his shoulder. "Where are you going?"

"Matau does not inspire a great deal of confidence," the Toa of Ice replied. "The Vahki may not listen to him. I am going to join him, and together we will —"

"I'm not surprised," said Nokama. "You are the one who is always talking about the virtues of teamwork, after all. How Toa Metru should always stay together and what folly it is for one to go off alone."

"Exactly," Nuju nodded. "I will be back once I have found Matau and we have completed our mission."

This time, Vakama let Nuju go a few steps.

Then Matau suddenly dropped from the ceiling, landing right on top of the stunned Toa of Ice. "No need to quick-hurry! I am here. And so are you, Krahka."

Matau pinned the Krahka to the floor. She snarled and squirmed, but the Toa of Air's grip would not be broken. Finally, the creature gave up the struggle and simply stared at her captors, with a mix of anger and respect in her eyes.

"Very clever," the Krahka said. "Here I just finished telling someone you were too trusting."

"There's a difference between trusting and stupid," replied Vakama. "We suspected you might try to deceive us again, so we set a trap of our own. And for your information, Nuju would rather shovel out Ussal crab stalls than take a long journey with Matau."

The Toa of Air hauled the Krahka to her feet, saying, "That's right. You underestimated how much Nuju cannot stand to be around . . ." His voice trailed off as he realized what he was saying.

"Now you are going to take us to Whenua

and Nuju," Onewa said to their captive. "No tricks. No transformations."

The Krahka said nothing in response, but the mask she wore smiled. Then her entire body began to shimmer and fade, as the Toa for the first time watched her change forms. In an instant, "Nuju" was gone, replaced by a monstrous lava eel. Matau jumped back with a cry as the skin of the creature turned blazing hot.

Free now, the Krahka slithered rapidly into a tunnel, leaving behind a scorched and smoking trail.

"Mata Nui," whispered Nokama. "How . . . how do we stop something that can do that?"

"I don't know," said Vakama. "But for the sake of Whenua and Nuju, we had better find a way."

The four Toa Metru followed the trail of the Krahka/lava eel for a long distance, before it suddenly vanished. Evidently tired of that form, the Krahka had switched to another that left no trace.

"Now how do we find her?" asked Vakama, frustrated.

"Maybe by *not* seek-finding her," said Matau. "Make sense?"

Onewa smiled. "Yes. It does. If we were to find an exit to the Archives —"

"She would have to do something to stop us," Nokama concluded. "You saw how she reacted to the thought of Vahki down here. She can't afford to let us escape. But how do we find a hatch in this maze?"

"We don't," said Onewa. "We make one. And we make lots of noise doing it."

Finding a spot with a relatively low ceiling, the Toa set to work. Vakama used some of his fading power to soften the stone, and then the other three went to work with their tools. It was slow going and there was no way to know how many feet of rock they would have to go through to reach the Archives. But none of them expected they would be allowed to complete the job anyway.

Vakama was the first to notice something

unusual. Out of the corner of his eye, he thought he saw a shadow move. He turned to get a better look. It wasn't a shadow, but a long tendril of black smoke snaking into the tunnel. It was followed by another and another, until it looked like some dark, tentacled beast floating in the air.

"She's here," he said very quietly to the others. All of them kept working as if they had not noticed anything. It was a risky strategy. If the Krahka had come to defeat them once and for all, allowing her to strike first would be a colossal mistake. But if there was a possibity she would take them back to her lair, where Nuju and Whenua would be waiting, then it was a risk they had to take.

Moving with the speed of an angry swarm of Nui-Rama insects, the tendrils wrapped themselves around the Toa. Each was enveloped in black smoke, able to breathe but not to see, hear, or move. Then came a sensation of weightlessness, as the Krahka lifted the Toa into the air and sent them floating through the tunnels.

If she could have, the Krahka would have

smiled over the ease of her victory. But monsters made of smoke don't have mouths to smile with, so her celebration would have to wait until she had changed forms once more. This thought did not bother her. After all, with the Toa Metru her helpless prisoners, she had all the time in the world.

Too bad the Toa cannot say the same, she said to herself.

The Toa Metru found themselves dumped on a cold stone floor like so many broken masks. They looked around to see they were in the same chamber where Whenua and now Nuju were held. The creature of smoke had disappeared, to be replaced by the form of Nokama.

"I do not like these bodies," the Krahka said. "But Rahkshi do not have the ability to speak your language. And I think it only right that you should know your fate."

"Why must we be enemies?" asked Vakama. "We came down here only to —"

"You came down to invade my home!" snapped the Krahka. "Just like all the other top-dwellers, with your drills, and your scraping tools, and your fires. Now I know that as long as there are dwellers up above, there will be no peace here."

The Nokama/Krahka's right arm suddenly shifted into a long, leather-scaled limb with nasty claws. "Have you ever seen the creature this belongs to? No, of course not. This Rahi produces a living crystal to weave its nest, a crystal that regenerates when damaged. In a few moments, I will use that crystal to seal off the exits to this chamber."

Then, still in Nokama's gentle voice, the Krahka added, "You six will remain here forever."

"There's an entire city up there," said Onewa. "Thousands of Matoran. Six Toa more or less won't stop them from coming down to these tunnels."

"But I want them to come," the Krahka hissed. "I want them all to come. Oh, at first I thought I could use your forms to keep them away, but now I realize that's a foolish idea. Better to lure them all down below the surface . . . and imprison them here . . . then make the land above my new home."

The Krahka's body began to shift into the form of a massive, hideous Rahi. As her head changed from Nokama's to the creature's, she said, "You cannot stop me. I have all your powers, all your skills. Accept your defeat, Toa Metru."

Fully transformed, the Krahka slithered away to begin sealing the first exit. Nokama turned to Onewa and whispered, "She may be right. She possesses our powers at full strength, while our energies are low."

"I might have an idea, but it needs all six of us to make it work," said the Toa of Stone. "I can free Nuju, given time, but what about Whenua?"

Matau pointed up to where the Toa of Earth was trapped. "I think he is quick-solving the problem for us. Look."

High above, Whenua had been working on his bonds tirelessly. The combination of his efforts and the intense heat from the protodermis pool down below had weakened the strands until they began to detach from the ceiling. Soon, they would be unable to support his weight. Of course, the bad news was that freedom would send him plummeting into molten protodermis.

"Any disks left?" Onewa asked Vakama.

"One. Not sure what good it will do against a shapeshifter, though."

"When Whenua falls, launch it. Matau?"

The Toa of Air had already readied his tools. At his mental signal, they would carry him into the air. He gestured up, across, and down to tell Onewa his plan.

"Can your hydro blades crack rock?" Vakama asked Nokama.

"Just watch them. Get ready."

Whenua had loosed his restraints enough to brace his feet against the ceiling. Now he gave one final shove and tore his bonds loose. The instant he saw the Toa of Earth begin to fall, Matau rocketed into the air.

Vakama loaded and launched in one smooth motion. The disk struck the Krahka and unleashed its power to reconstitute at random. The Rahi bellowed with rage as her body went through multiple changes at once, arms and legs shifting rapidly from one form to another.

Onewa and Nokama moved so fast it almost looked as if they had been hurled from a launcher as well. They vaulted over the proto-dermis pool and struck Nuju's stone prison as one. Onewa's knowledge of stone served him well, as his proto pitons found just the right weak point to hit. The rock cracked down the middle and fell apart, freeing the Toa of Ice.

Up above, Matau caught Whenua before he had fallen too far. Rather than fight to stay aloft carrying the extra weight, the Toa of Air went into a power dive, heading right for the Krahka. But the Rahi spotted the danger and used Vakama's powers to throw up a wall of flame in their path.

The Toa of Fire had no time to think, only to act. He flung out his arms and strained to absorb the fire into him. If he failed, Whenua and Matau were doomed.

Nokama, Onewa, and Nuju watched from the other side of the chamber, knowing they were helpless to aid him. Matau and Whenua were only seconds from plunging into the flames.

Where Vakama found the strength of will, he would never know. But suddenly the flames began to whirl like a cyclone and shot across the room into the Toa of Fire. Glowing with power, he unleashed them again at the wall behind the Krahka, blasting it into rubble.

"Try sealing that up," he shouted.

Rattled by the explosion, the Krahka could not get out of the way of the diving Toa. But she transformed by reflex into a gelatinous creature, and Whenua and Matau shot right through her and landed hard on the floor. The Krahka shifted again, this time into a purple Rahkshi, then let out a scream.

The force of the yell knocked the Toa off their feet. Vakama, drained from his efforts against the wall of flame, flew halfway across the chamber. Matau and Whenua tried to rise, but a second scream slammed them into the wall.

The Krahka's form changed once more, this time into the shape of Vakama. But she was clearly beginning to tire. "You . . . have no idea . . . what you are dealing with," she said. "There are things down here . . . things I have seen . . . that dwarf your power. If I become one,

I could down you all with one blow and then crush your city."

Vakama saw the Rahi wearing his form and heard the words coming out of "his" mouth. His rage overcame his weakness. He rose and began striding across the chamber toward the Krahka. "Then do it!" he shouted. "Show us your power, if you can!"

Nokama started forward. "Vakama —"

Nuju blocked her path. "No, let him speak. While her attention is on him, we can help Matau and Whenua. Then the Toa Metru will stand united."

"And we know how much you like that," Onewa said, smiling at Nuju.

"It has its place," was all the Toa of Ice said.

Vakama had not slowed in his march toward the Rahi. The Krahka took a step backward, saying, "You think you can stand against my power? You are a fool, Toa of Fire!"

"And you are a thief!" snapped Vakama. "Not a conqueror — just a pathetic creature who survives by stealing the might of others, because she has none of her own. Maybe you started out wanting only to protect your home, Krahka, but it has made you into a monster."

The other Toa had thought Vakama was only trying to distract the Rahi. But as they moved to surround her, they saw he had not even noticed them. His attention and anger were focused on her, and hers on him.

The Krahka shouted something in a language none had ever heard and launched beams of fire and ice at Vakama. Amazingly, he did not even try to dodge. It was as if the emotions inside him were acting as a shield against her powers.

"You may defeat us all," he said. "You may defeat every Matoran and every Vahki in all of Metru Nui. But you will not do it looking like a Toa. You will not shame what a Toa stands for, or one who has fallen to protect our city. That I swear!"

The Krahka looked around, finally noticing that the other five Toa were closing in. But she showed no fear or hesitation. Instead, she laughed and said, "Not as a Toa? Very well, then —"

Now began the most amazing transformation of all. Before the horrified eyes of the Toa Metru, the Krahka grew and changed into a walking nightmare. No longer was she Vakama, or any single Toa. Now she towered above them as a frightening combination of all six.

A fearsome face smiled down at them. Six arms slowly waved in the air as she grew accustomed to her new form. "Do you like this better, little ones?" she said, her voice the mingled tones of all the Toa Metru.

"There's an exhibit for the Archives, librarian," said Onewa.

"I don't think she will fit," Whenua replied. "Outside of running away, anyone have any good ideas?"

"Spread out," said Vakama. "Let's not make it easy for her."

"Are we escaping?" asked Whenua.

"No," answered Nuju as he readied his crystal spikes. "We are ending this."

"Ah," said Matau, aero slicers in his hands. "Well, I had no thought-plans for today, anyway."

The Krahka watched with amusement as

the Toa Metru took up positions around her. Every move she made in her new combined form filled the Toa with revulsion. But it was Nokama who first took a step forward.

"Beware, Toa of Water," rumbled the Krahka. "Even you cannot withstand Vakama's flames."

"No, I can't," Nokama agreed. "Can you? You have gone too far, Krahka. I think you know it, too. If you have our power, don't you have our wisdom as well? Does this have to end in battle?"

"Yes! You must fall! The mask-makers must be driven from the Sculpture Fields. The knowledge crystals must not fly through the chutes. And . . . and the exhibits . . . they must be purified . . . and stored . . . so that the canals can flow . . ."

The Krahka swayed, as the images and knowledge derived from six minds flooded her own. For a moment, it seemed as if would be too much, and Nokama was certain victory was at hand. But the Krahka's will was too strong. She steadied herself again.

"You would have lived out your lives here,

safe from harm," the Krahka said, raising all six of her arms. "But now . . ."

The Toa Metru knew what was coming. Their only hope was to move fast. Together, the heroes of Metru Nui charged.

Raw power surged from within the Krahka. Bolts of ice and fire, storms of earth and stone, whirlpools of water and air rained down on the Toa. They struggled to make headway against their own power, only to be driven back. With their full energies, they might have achieved a stalemate. Weakened as they were, it seemed they could not win.

Vakama, half frozen by Nuju's power, glanced up at the Krahka. He expected to see a creature aglow with triumph as she drove the Toa down. But instead the Krahka looked as if she were about to collapse.

"Keep struggling!" he shouted to the other Toa. "Don't give in!"

The Krahka unleashed more and more power. One by one, the Toa Metru fell before the onslaught, only to somehow find the strength to rise again. The Krahka's fury grew greater every moment, but all her might could not make the Toa surrender.

Far below, the Toa struggled for their very lives. Nuju battled to make headway against raging winds; Nokama leaped and dodged white-hot fireballs; Matau batted stones away with his aero slicers; Vakama pressed on through a howling blizzard; Onewa fought to overcome tidal waves of earth as Whenua did the same with water.

The Toa of Water realized there was no way to overcome the Krahka with sheer might. The only hope for victory lay in striking out at the Rahi's willpower and weaken her from within.

"I hope you win!" Nokama shouted at the Krahka. "It will be the fate you deserve!"

The Krahka's attack did not slow, but she regarded the Toa with puzzlement.

Nuju guessed Nokama's plan and decided it was a good one. "She right!" he shouted over the wind. "At least if we are trapped here, we will be together. You will be alone for eternity, Krahka."

Nokama barely dodged the hottest fireball

yet. "I've seen how the Rahkshi are around you. They fear you, just like everything else down here. They know you for a deceiver."

"The Rahi will flee Metru Nui," Onewa added. "You will be the absolute ruler of . . . nothing."

The Krahka did not take this suggestion well. She began combining her powers in one blast, using earth and water to bury Onewa in a sea of mud. Nokama needed all her agility to avoid molten rock. Vakama faced a blizzard of snow, ice, and stone.

"We will build a new city-home down here," said Matau. "But even in the suns' light, monster, you will always be in night-dark!"

"You are trying to confuse me!" bellowed the Krahka. "It will not work!"

Whenua could see she was lying. Better still, she was expending huge amounts of power as she grew more agitated. Onewa had told him something of how the Krahka had used his form to fool the Toa, so Whenua decided it was time for payback.

Fighting the crushing might of the water, he bent down and activated his earthshock drills. Their sound could not be heard over the winds in the chamber. He swiftly dug a hole and dove into it, followed by the waters. If he was right, this maneuver would shake the Krahka up even more. If he was wrong, there would only be five Toa left to fight.

The massive Rahi noticed immediately that Whenua was gone. "Where? Where is the Toa of Earth?" she demanded, casting her eyes about frantically.

The stone floor behind the Krahka exploded. Whenua's head emerged from the hole. "Surprise!" he yelled. "See what a real Toa of Earth can do, not some cheap imitation!"

Whenua vanished underground again. Enraged, the Krahka melted the stone around the hole, all the while continuing to fend off the other five Toa.

Down below, the Toa of Earth fought to hold his breath as his drills carved through the stone.

If he was right the Krahka was just above him, and about to get a shock.

The Krahka felt the ground give way beneath her and struggled to keep her balance. She would not fall before these . . . these interlopers! She would crush them here and now, and then all top-dwellers, and she would rule above! But . . . who would she rule? Mindless Rahi? And what would she have them do?

No, it didn't matter. They would obey her commands. And her first command would be to . . . to . . .

But what if they all fled at her approach? Then she would stop them. She would imprison them in the city, just like she had done the top-dwellers. She would cage everything that existed—only that way could she be sure of her own survival.

As her inner debate raged, the Toa were able to make progress against her weakening powers. Onewa could sense that the end was near, if only one more event would push her over the edge. He signaled for the Toa to move closer together and form a wedge, forcing the Krahka to focus maximum power on one spot.

Reacting to their maneuver, the Krahka pointed her six arms all in one direction and brought the powers bursts near to each other. At the crucial moment, Whenua tore out of the ground behind her, his shout of rage breaking her concentration. The elemental energies she wielded merged together in that one instant into one awesome blast.

The Toa narrowly ducked the power beam. Only Vakama turned to see that where it struck a new substance had formed, one that looked like solid protodermis. *How could that be?* he wondered. *Is that what would result if we combined out powers?* Maybe—

"Vakama, watch out!" Nokama shouted.

Then, without warning, the power ceased to flow from the hands of the Krahka. The giant Rahi staggered and fell, slamming into the ground with such force that surely all of Metru Nui must have trembled. She lay still, her body slowly beginning another tranformation, but into what, none could tell.

Vakama approached the prone form. "She still lives. Trying to use all our powers at once overwhelmed her. It is over . . . for now."

"Yes, for now," said Nokama. "But what, cage could hope to hold a creature that can transform at will?"

"The Onu-Matoran can put her in stasis," offered Whenua. "She can be kept in the Archives until it is safe, someday, to release her."

"And if there are more like her down here?" said Onewa.

"That is the Toa of Stone," said Matau. "Always with the happy-cheer."

"No!" groaned the Krahka. "No . . . I will not be . . . chained!"

The Toa whirled to see their opponent had shifted to the form of a lava eel once more. Only Vakama was close enough to stop her, but he did not move as she plunged into the pool of molten protodermis. The others ran to the edge of the pool, but there was no sign of her.

"Why didn't you stop her?" demanded Onewa. "You just let her go!"

"She fought to protect her home. But too much power, fueled by too much anger, made her a menace," Vakama said quietly. "Perhaps I saw a reflection of ourselves in her . . . of what we could become, if we are not very careful."

Onewa threw up his hands. "Someday I will figure you out, fire-spitter. But not today, it seems."

Nokama stared at the molten pool for a long time. Had Vakama done the right thing? The Krahka was no unthinking beast, but she did have a great deal to learn before she could live in peace with others. Still, could any being hope to master such lessons in a cage? The Toa of Water could not say for sure. But one question more haunted her. . . . With its power to change shapes, if the Krahka did survive and someday re-turned . . . how would they know?

EPILOGUE

His tale finished, Turaga Vakama sat down. Tahu Nuva was the first to speak. "I see that the shape of victory was perhaps not so easy to recognize on Metru Nui, as it has been here. Still, I am sure the Matoran applauded your achievements."

Vakama shook his head. "They were never to hear this story, Toa of Fire. We sealed the cracks we had come to find, then departed from the tunnels. On the way, we decided that it would serve no purpose to share our experiences with others. Whenua offered to warn the Matoran to be careful where they dug in future, to avoid harming the natural life below."

"But if it was a menace —?" said Kopaka Nuva.

"It was defending its home against an invader, much as you did against the Bohrok," replied Vakama. "Now that it knew that one could not hope to defeat six, it would not threaten the surface world again. Or so we believed . . ."

"That, then, is the lesson of this tale," said Hahli. "When the Toa stand together, no force can overcome them."

Vakama gave the Chronicler a smile of approval. "Very good. That is half the lesson learned. What is the rest?"

Hahli had no answer. The Toa Nuva looked at each other, equally puzzled. Finally, Lewa spoke up. "Stay topside. The underground is a nasty-dark place."

The Toa Nuva — even Kopaka — had to smile at that. Vakama chuckled and said, "No, Toa of Air, although there is truth in that as well. We learned it is not enough just to trust — one must trust wisely. Nuju trusted the sight of Nokama and so wound up in an embrace of stone. The

The Darkness Below

Krahka took our friendship and our reliance upon each other and used it as a tool against us."

The Turaga of Fire leaned forward and spoke with quiet urgency. "Trust not in what you see and hear, Toa Nuva. Trust in what your mind and heart tell you. That is something which, even after this adventure, the Toa Metru had still not grasped completely."

Vakama's expression turned grim. "And it is a lesson that cost us dearly. Very dearly."

"So what happened next?" asked Jaller. "Did you ever make it to the Coliseum? Were you recognized as heroes?"

"After we emerged from the tunnels, we decided to return to our own metru briefly to ensure our Matoran friends were safe. We also needed to secure some of the loose ends of our old lives before leaving them behind forever. Those are stories for another day. But, yes, we did finally come to the Coliseum to present ourselves to Turaga Dume and the Matoran assembled."

"And —?" asked Taka Nuva, Toa of Light, eagerly.

"I can see you will not be content until you have heard the tale in full," Vakama said softly. "Very well, my friends. I will share with you the legends of Metru Nui . . ."

The Turaga would talk long into the night, recalling for the Toa Nuva a world they had never known.

BUILD AN EXCLUSIVE BIONICLE MODEL!

On the following pages you'll find photographs of a Bionicle. You won't find this particular kit in a store. This Bionicle was built by combining different sets. Use the photos as inspiration and see what you can create with your own collection!

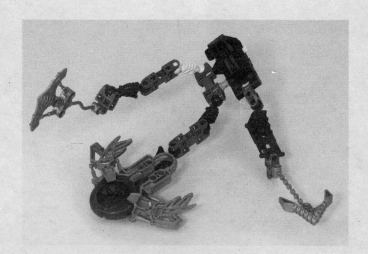